Contents

THE CAST

KING ARTIE

QUEEN GWINNY

THE KNIGHTS

SIR PRANCELOT . . . . the keen one

SIR PERCY . . . . the fussy one

SIR GARY . . . . the gloomy one

SIR TRALAHAD . . . . the musical one

SIR BORE DE GANNET . . . ze French one

SIR ANGELA . . . . she's a girl in disguise

THE STAFF

OLD TOBY . . . . the gardener

SHAWN . . . . the odd job boy

MRS SPUNGE . . . . the cook

AGGIE . . . . the serving wench

THE CASTLE ANIMALS

ETHEL . . . . the cat

BOB . . . . the dog

THE HORSES

STOP-A-LOT . . . . who stops a lot

LIGHTNING . . . . the slow one

BREAKWIND . . . . don't stand behind him

ELTON . . . . she's a mare

LOUD WINNIE . . . . the noisy one

GNASHER . . . . he bites

Prologue

It was lunch time at Castle Llamalot. The King was tucking into a big boar burger and chips. The Queen was picking at a plate of peacock fritters. Bob, the castle dog, lay under the table. He hoped some titbits might drop his way.

"So," the King said, as he dabbed his moustache with a napkin. "How is the knights' new room working out, darling? Any complaints?"

"Rather to my surprise, no," the Queen said. "There was the odd problem at first, of course. The table gave a bit of trouble. It collapsed in the middle of their very first all knight party. But then, all drop-leafs do that. We didn't have a spare round one, and a drop-leaf table was the best I could do."

"Well, it was an excellent idea, Gwinny," the King said. "Clever old you, to give the knights a room of their own. Wonderful."

"Thank you, Artie," the Queen said. "I must say it is a lot more peaceful without them clanking up and down the castle corridors. But goodness knows what they do in their room all day. Aggie asked Angela – I mean, Sir AnGela – and she – *he*, I mean, *he* said, "Argue."

"Good, good," the King said, and he reached for the paper. His eye had caught a headline and he was fast losing interest in the knights.

"Old Toby fixed the table with a pot of Kwicky-Sticky and it seems to be holding," the Queen said. "Cook sends Aggie in with tea and biscuits every day. Aggie says that in between arguing they're talking about going on a quest."

"Mmm?"

"I said, they're planning a quest."

"Good, good. Excellent."

"You're doing the sudoku, Artie. You're not listening."

"Oh, I am, I am," the King said. "They're planning what?"

"A quest. A competition to find out who's the bravest and noblest. They will award points and the one with the most points gets a prize."

"A prize?" the King said. "What prize?"

"I think they want us to supply that," the Queen said with a sigh. "I thought I'd offer them an old silver goblet. We've got a whole box full of them up in the loft."

"Well, as long as I'm not involved," the King said, with his nose back in the paper. "Have one of my chips, darling. You know you want to."

Chapter 1

The Knights

"So," Sir Percy said. "The New Register." He opened the red folder with a grand flourish. "All names are in order from A to Z. When I call yours, you will answer in one of three ways. 1. 'Yes.' 2. 'Here.' 3. 'Present.' Is that clear?"

Silence. The other knights stared. A register? This was new. Nobody had asked for a register.

"Who says we want a register?" asked Sir Gary. "I know *I* don't."

"Well, we need one," Sir Percy said. "So I decided to make one for us. I was up all night, as a matter of fact."

"Awesome!" Sir Prancelot cried, with a toss of his long fair hair. "Huzzah! Three cheers for the noble Sir Percy and his splendid New Register! Hip, hip –"

Stony silence. Stares. No one said a word.

"Oh," said Sir Prancelot. "Just me, then."

"There's only six of us. Why do we need a register?" asked Sir Angela, who was a girl.

Nobody said anything, because one of the rules of the Code of Chivalry was that you had to be polite to girls. Everyone said her name with a hard G, like in Garden, and they all pretended not to notice that her moustache was drawn on.

"So that we have a proper record of who's here on what day, of course," said Sir Percy, and dipped his quill pen in an ink pot. "Angela? I mean, Sir AnGela?"

"What?" Sir Angela said.

"Are you here?"

"You know I'm here. I'm talking to you."

"Kindly answer 'Yes', 'Here' or 'Present'."

"Yes, then."

"Thank you." Sir Percy ticked off Sir Angela's name. "Sir Bore de Gannet?"

"*Oui*," said Sir Bore de Gannet, who was French. "*Je suis ici*. Yes, I am 'ere."

"No need for the *français*," Sir Percy said. "Olde English will do. Sir Gary?"

"No," said Sir Gary. He liked to be awkward. "I'm away drinking tea with the Queen of the Fairies."

"I'll take that as a yes," Sir Percy said. "I'm next. As you can see, I am indeed fully present. Sir Prancelot?"

"Yah!" Sir Prancelot cried. "Absolutely! It's a clear yes from me!"

"Thank you. And lastly, Sir Tralahad."

"Here," said Sir Tralahad, who was busy stringing his lyre with new strings. "Can we get on now? I thought we were here to discuss The Quest."

"Yah!" Sir Prancelot burst out. He leaped to his feet, took out his sword and waved it around his head. "The Quest. Yep-a-doodle-doo!"

"Careful!" everybody cried as the table wobbled. The drop-leaf side was stuck in place with Kwicky-Sticky, but nobody trusted it yet.

"Not only did I prepare the register," Sir Percy said, "I thought ahead too. Shawn! My next surprise, if you please!"

Shawn, the odd job boy, kicked the door open and stepped into the room. He had a grumpy look on his face and he was holding the next surprise.

"A blackboard," Sir Percy said. "So we can make notes about The Quest. Put it over there, Shawn, and go."

With a scowl, Shawn put it over there and went.

"Ooo!" Sir Gary sneered at Sir Percy. "You *have* been a busy boy."

Sir Percy ignored him. He clanked over to the blackboard and took a stick of chalk from a small metal pocket in his breast plate.

"Right. Now, we all agree to go on solo quests, right? No questing in pairs and no conferring."

There came a general *clank clank clank* as helmeted heads nodded.

"So, the first question is, how long for? Today's Monday. I feel that three days is about right. Plenty of time to get far enough away to do what we have to do, but not so much time that we'll need a bath and a change of armour."

"Rain's forecast for Thursday," Sir Tralahad piped up. "We need to be back by then."

Everyone nodded again. Armour and rain are so not a good combo.

"Three days it is, then," Sir Percy said. He used his new chalk to write on the blackboard –

Quest lenth – 3 days.

"There's a G in length," Sir Angela said, helpfully.

"What about the points?" Sir Prancelot asked. "Oh, *please* can we talk about the points, guys? I've been thinking about this for *ever*. I reckon it should be the maximum 10 points for fighting a dragon and scooping up the jolly old treasure! Thrills, spills, fire, sword play, bags of gold, plenty of cave action. Nothing can top it in quest terms, am I right?"

He was right. To kill a dragon and ride home with a load of treasure was as questy as a quest could get.

"Agreed," Sir Percy said, a bit miffed because he hadn't got there first. "I was about to say that myself."

He wrote –

Fight dragon and get treser – 10 points.

"You've spelled treasure wrong," Sir Angela pointed out, as helpful as ever. "It's *t r e a s u r e*."

"Yes, well, let's stick to the point, shall we?" Sir Percy said. "Or, *points*, rather. What do we think wins 9 points?"

"A rescue of ze damsels in distress," Sir Bore de Gannet said. He had a French accent, an interest in fine food and interesting facial hair. He thought of himself as a bit of a ladies' man.

"Why?" Sir Gary demanded. "They get themselves into distress, let 'em get themselves out."

"Tut tut, sir! Remember the Code of Chivalry!" Sir Prancelot scolded. "We must give the gals a hand in their time of need. It's 9 points for the damsels, Sir Percy! All who agree say 'Aye'."

All but Sir Gary and Sir Angela said "Aye".

And so Sir Percy wrote –

~~rescew resku reks~~ helping damsels in distres – 9 points

"Distress has two s's at the end," Sir Angela pointed out.

"Dis dress, dat dress, who cares what the silly girls are wearing?" Sir Gary said.

Everyone ignored him.

"I suggest 8 points for finding ze sword in ze stone!" Sir Bore de Gannet said.

"Yah! And 7 for one in a lake!" Sir Prancelot shouted.

"And 6 for a sword up a treeeeee," Sir Tralahad sang as he plucked at his lyre. "And 5 for one under a bush, tra-la-LA!"

"And 4 for one stuck down the side of the sofa," said Sir Angela. She added, "That's enough swords. Something else."

Sir Prancelot waved his arm in the air. "Guys! Guys! I have it!"

"Yes?" Sir Percy asked, his voice tired. In his opinion, Sir Prancelot had rather too much to say.

"I propose 3 points for being jolly kind to a grubby old peasant in disguise who turns out to be a wise woman who rewards us with a magic amulet that will protect us in battle!"

"Like heck it will," Sir Gary said.

"Well, it *is* a noble deed to be kind to peasants," Sir Percy said. "I was about to propose that myself."

"What about finding lost pets and returning them to their owners?" Sir Tralahad called out. "For a dog, 2 points. And 1 point for a cat."

"It should be the other way round," said Sir Angela, who was a cat lover.

"Slow down, slow down," Sir Percy said. "I need to write all this down."

"Nah you don't," said Sir Gary. He leaned over, grabbed Sir Percy's chalk and dropped it on the floor, where it broke. "Enough writing, it's boring."

"I have a good mind to call you out for that, sir!" Sir Percy said.

"Go on, then," said Sir Gary.

Luckily, just then, Aggie the serving wench arrived with the tea, and that stopped the knight fight in its tracks.

"Could you ask Mrs Spunge if she could make us some sandwiches, please, Aggie?" Sir Angela asked as Aggie set the tray on the table. The drop-leaf half sagged a bit. "Three days' worth, if it's no trouble. We're off on The Quest this afternoon. After lunch."

"Certainly, miss– sir," said Aggie. "Um – is this the one where you get points?"

"It is, young woman," Sir Percy said. "He who has the best quest will score the most points and will therefore win an actual prize. The Queen sent a note about it this morning. It says –

"May the best knight win. On your return, I will present the winner with a silver goblet. Good luck to you all. Yours royally, The Queen."

"That's a nice prize," Sir Angela said. "I was expecting a box of chocolates."

"A silver goblet!" Sir Prancelot cried, leaping to his feet. "Three cheers for Her Majesty! Hip, hip –"

This time, everyone joined in. After all, everyone loved the Queen.

Chapter 2
Setting Off

Old Toby the gardener and Shawn the odd job boy sat on two water butts in the stable yard. They were both fed up. It had taken them all morning to groom, saddle up and decorate six entire horses. The horses hadn't taken it well and had all been awkward in their own special way.

Now – at last – all six were kitted out in their best tassels and plumes and shiny bits and cloths of all different colours. They stood in their stable, swishing their tails and nibbling on hay. They were tired out from being awkward and needed to get their second wind.

The knights stood in a circle in the middle of the yard. Sir Percy had taken off his helmet and now held it upside down.

"So," he said. "Same as always. Six slips of paper with our names on. No moaning. Pass it round."

The helmet was passed round and everyone took a slip. They unfolded them and a chorus of groans broke out.

"Oh, no! Pur-leeese! Not Stop-A-Lot. I had him last time."

"Breakwind *again*? I don't believe it!"

"I've got Gnasher! How unfair is that?"

"Alors! Zis is bad. I 'ave Loud Winnie. 'Fetch ze ear plugs!"

"Lightning? Are you *serious*? Snails are quicker."

The only one who looked happy was Sir Angela, who had picked Elton – a good-tempered mare with no major defects.

"Don't just sit there!" Sir Percy snapped at Old Toby and Shawn. "Fetch the horses."

Old Toby and Shawn tramped over to the stable, where all the horses except Elton began to whinny, snort, eye-roll, head toss, kick and lean sideways. All of which gave Old Toby and Shawn another hard time.

Just then, Aggie arrived with a basket full of sandwiches. The knights crowded around.

Sir Tralahad sang –

"Hey nonny no, when it
comes to the crunch,
There's nothing compares
to a fine packed lunch!"

And everyone agreed.

"There's roast royal swan, stag and cress, cold boar and mustard, griffin salad and peacock and pickle," Aggie told them. "Three packs each, one for each day. Three sandwiches to a pack. Nine in total. Mrs Spunge says don't eat them all at once, you'll be sorry at supper time. Who's for what?"

The knights picked their sandwiches without too much bickering. Sir Bore de Gannet was cross that there were no croissants. Sir Gary didn't fancy any of them.

"One more thing we need to discuss before we depart," Sir Percy said as they clanked over to the horses. "Proof. We must bring back proof of our brave and noble deeds. No proof, no points. No points, no prize."

"A True Knight Never Lies," Sir Prancelot said. "Our word should be proof enough. Right, guys?"

No one looked convinced.

"I don't trust any of you," Sir Gary said. "I'll *certainly* need to see proof."

"Then I trust the mighty head of a dragon will convince you, sir!" Sir Prancelot cried. Sir Gary was starting to grind his gears now. "Because *that* shall be my proof!"

"How will I know it was you who chopped it off? You might have just found it on the floor," Sir Gary said.

"Ignore him," Sir Angela said to Sir Prancelot. "He's winding you up."

"Treasure and swords and magic amulets speak for themselves, don't they?" Sir Tralahad said. "They're easy to bring home."

"But what about ze damsels?" Sir Bore de Gannet asked. "Zey might not want to come all ze way back 'ere. Zey might want to go and see zair mum and wash zair 'air."

"They can write a note," Sir Angela said. "For example –

I, Lady Sissy SoppyPants, being totally feeble and pathetic, confirm that this is the knight that rescued me, a damsel, from distress."

"What about the lost pets?" Sir Tralahad asked. "They'll be back with their owners, won't they?"

"More notes," Sir Angela said. **"This is the knight that found my dog. Signed – a happy owner.** Look, are we questing or not? Time moves on, you know. We need to get some miles in before sunset."

There followed a lot of fuss and bother as everyone clanked to their horse and tried to get on. As always, the horses backed away, screeched, clashed their hooves, trod on feet, leaned the wrong way, nipped and were as awkward as awkward can be.

All except Elton, who waited nicely while Sir Angela got into the saddle.

"I'm going west," Sir Angela shouted as she took the reins. "See you in three days!"

She clicked to Elton and rode out of the yard.

"She's – he's got a head start!" Sir Percy cried. "That's so not fair."

Sir Percy had been trying to put his foot in the stirrup of the worst horse of all. The worst horse of all was Gnasher and he was a proper biter. You had to get on him very, very carefully, when his head with its massive yellow teeth was facing the other way.

"Ah – stand *up*, will you! You're jolly well annoying me now!" Sir Prancelot protested. His horse was Stop-A-Lot – a laidback horse who liked to stop, chew on the long grass and take his time to go anywhere. Fancy horse armour didn't suit Stop-A-Lot. He would have looked better in a floppy sun hat. It was hard to get up on him, because he was leaning on the stable door as he chewed a long strand of straw.

Sir Tralahad had Breakwind, who no one ever wanted to ride. Sir Tralahad was a musical knight and he liked to sing as he rode. Breakwind's own loud bottom music drowned him out. Breakwind came with a clothes peg to clip over your nose. It hung on a silver chain round his neck.

Sir Bore de Gannet had Loud Winnie. She didn't so much neigh as screech. A quiet canter through the woods was impossible with Winnie. She was so loud that you had to stuff cotton wool in your ears. Old Toby kept a handy roll of it in the shed.

That left Sir Gary with Lightning, who never ever galloped, didn't canter, hated to trot and kept to a slow, sulky shuffle. Knight and horse stared at each other in gloomy dislike, then each gave a shrug and looked away.

Old Toby and Shawn ran around doing what they could – a boost up here and a yank on a rein there. But they couldn't be everywhere at once, and it took time before everyone was up on his horse and facing the right way, feet in stirrups, reins in hand and three days' worth of sandwiches packed in the saddlebags.

"Glad that's over," Old Toby said to Shawn as they watched the knights ride out of the yard and down the lane to the forest. "Bit of peace at last."

"How long are they going for?" Shawn asked.

"Three days," Aggie said. She'd waited around to watch the knights leave. "Back by Thursday."

"No chance," Old Toby said. "They'll be back long before then. Soon as they've run out of sandwiches. You mark my words."

Chapter 3

A Wise Woman and a Damsel

Sir Angela was off to a good start, and she knew it. It was excellent luck to be paired with Elton. The horse moved along under the trees, head held high, lively hooves pounding the forest floor, fast but not too fast. They were a good ten minutes in front of the others.

As they rode, Sir Angela thought. She needed a plan. She was tempted to go for the maximum 10 points and bag herself a dragon's head. On the other hand, dragons lived in mountain caves and the nearest mountain was on the other side of the forest. What if there was only one dragon and one of the others got there first? Unlikely, but possible.

Plus, Sir Angela was an animal lover. And she wasn't a big fan of blood and gore. She didn't much fancy cutting the head off an actual dragon.

She'd score high marks for a damsel in distress, but that was out. Sir Angela agreed with Sir Gary. Damsels in distress should help themselves, not hang around waiting for some random knight or prince to rescue them. Sir Angela would never put up with such nonsense. Not even for 9 points.

It would be good to find a sword – in a stone, a lake, a tree, anywhere at all. She would keep an eye open. It was unlikely, of course. Swords didn't appear by magic. Well, they *did* – but not often. There was a pond in the forest, not far away, but Sir Angela didn't want to wait around just in case a hand with a sword lifted up out of the water. She'd score 7 points, but what were the chances? Big fat zero.

By now she had ridden for almost 15 minutes and it was time for the first sandwich break. Sir Angela knew she should wait – the sandwiches had to last three days – but right now, she wanted one and that was that. There is something about a packet of sandwiches that makes you desperate to get stuck in, even if you've only just had your lunch.

So Sir Angela reined in Elton, jumped down, took a packet from her saddlebag and clanked over to a log on the ground.

The packet contained three huge egg and cress sandwiches with a sprig of parsley on top. Mrs Spunge, the castle cook, couldn't make biscuits to save her life, but her sandwiches were BIG.

Sir Angela was about to take the first bite, when a voice in her ear rasped, "Are you eatin' all o' them?"

A bent, hooded stranger in a cloak was standing right behind her, leaning on a stick.

"What?" Sir Angela said as she clanked to her feet.

"I'm asking if you want 'em all?" the stranger said. "All of them massive sarnies?"

"Why?" Sir Angela asked. "Would you like one?"

"What are they?"

"Stag and cress. Without the stag. I asked for egg instead."

"Ain't you got boar and mustard?"

"No, sorry. I'm veggie."

"I'll give it a try," the stranger said.

They both sat down on the log. The stranger held out a grubby hand.

"Come on, hand it over."

"*Bon appetit!*" Sir Angela said, and they both chewed their sandwiches.

"So, what d'you think?" Sir Angela asked after a bit.

"All right. Could do with more mayo."

They chewed some more.

"Are you a wise woman in disguise?" Sir Angela asked. Well, it was worth a shot.

"Yep," the hooded stranger said. "But I'm not in disguise. I always look like this."

"Do you – I don't suppose – do you have any magic amulets on you?"

"In return for this sarnie, you mean?"

"Um – yes. I'm on a Quest, you see. We all are. We win points for good deeds."

"Oh. Right. Give us the other sarnie and we might be in business."

Sir Angela handed the third sandwich over. She was sad to see it go.

"Well now, let me think," the wise woman said. "Magic amulet, you say? You mean one o' those things you wear round yer neck?"

"Yes."

"Or dangle from yer helmet?"

"Yes, that's it."

"Supposed to keep you safe in battle?"

"Yes!"

"Come in different colours?"

"Yes! I don't know, maybe. Do you have one?"

"Nope. Right out."

"Oh," Sir Angela said. "That's a shame. Never mind."

"I can do you a bunch o' lucky white heather, if that's any good."

"Is white heather as lucky as an amulet?"

"Well, it's no worse."

"Yes please, then. That would be great."

The wise woman put her hand under her cloak and brought out a bunch of grubby white heather.

"There you go, miss– sir."

"Thanks a lot."

"That's all right. But I wouldn't rely on it. Its luckiness, I mean. Tell the truth, I've had it for a few years. I'm not even sure it's white. Could be purple gone all old and faded. Anyway, I'm off. Ta for the sarnies."

"You're welcome," Sir Angela said.

'Result!' she thought. 'Three points! A magic amulet would have been better, but lucky heather's the same. Isn't it?'

And she still had sandwiches for tomorrow and the next day.

*

Sir Tralahad rode on Breakwind, and as he rode, he sang.

The singing was rather odd because of the clothes peg on his nose, but Sir Tralahad was a true musician and sang no matter what. In particular, he sang when he was alone and didn't have to suffer rude comments from the other knights, who all had ears made of tin. He was working on a new song. He would call it *Quest-O!*

Sir Tralahad trilled, in his reedy voice –

"I'm going on a quest-o,
I've got my lucky vest-o
I've got my shiny helmet on
I think I look well dressed-o!

Quest-O! Quest-O!
A sort of knightly test-o,
With dragons and with fighting
And with girls who are distressed … oh!"

He broke off.

There, in a glade before him, stood a tower. Tall and straight, it rose high above the trees. At the top, there was a balcony – and dangling over the balcony was a mass of – was it? Yes! Hair! Long yellow hair which, he was pretty sure, belonged to a girl in a frilly pink dress who was eating an apple.

Sir Tralahad had heard all about beautiful damsels in distress who let their extra-long hair dangle down from the top of a tower. This was story-book stuff. Almost too good to be true.

He pulled on Breakwind's reins. You wouldn't want people to get down wind of Breakwind if you wanted to impress them.

Sir Tralahad took the clothes peg off his nose.

"What ho, fair lady!" he called. "Greetings on this splendid day! How beautiful you look, with the sunlight on your golden curls!"

The girl took the apple from her mouth, stared at Sir Tralahad and said,

"You what?"

"I was singing the praises of your hair. The silken locks that flow in the sunshine."

"That's not me hair, you dummy," the girl said. "That's the kitchen mat. I just washed it." She moved away from the 'golden curls'. "You need specs, mate."

Oh. It *was* too good to be true.

Sir Tralahad felt silly. He was short sighted, but he didn't want to wear specs. He was a free spirit, not a nerd. Specs made you look clever, but not artistic. Except dark glasses, but that was different.

He wondered whether to praise the girl's real hair, but decided not to. It was nothing special. He would move on. All was not yet lost.

"Are you in distress?" Sir Tralahad shouted up. "Are you locked in up there? Are you a prisoner of a wicked old witch or vile monster who is demanding a ransom from your rich father? Anything like that going on?"

"Is this a joke?" the girl said. "Are you taking the Michael?"

'Michael,' Sir Tralahad thought. 'Who's he?' But he said, "I just wondered if you need me to rescue you."

"No," the girl said. "I bloomin' well don't. Who are you anyway?"

"Ah. Of course. Let me introduce myself." Sir Tralahad took his helmet off with a sigh. It had been digging into the back of his neck. Looking up with a helmet on is not very comfortable. "I am Sir Tralahad, of Castle Llamalot. I'm on a Quest to right wrongs and I'm on the lookout for swords and damsels and dragons. I'm writing a song about it, in fact. It's called *Quest-O!* You can be in it if you like."

"What?"

"Lady, you see before you a poet-singer. See?" Sir Tralahad held up his lyre. "They call me *The Singing Knight*."

"Who do?"

Sir Tralahad thought. In fact, no one called him "The Singing Knight". He would have liked them to, but they didn't.

"People," he said. "My many fans."

"I bet you haven't got any fans," the girl said. "Mind you, you could do with a fan around that stinky horse."

"Tell me about it," Sir Tralahad said in a bitter voice. "I didn't choose him, you know."

"Well, I'd like you to ride away on him now." The girl gave a sniff. "Coming here in your tin suit with your daft ideas. Go on, clear off, before I call my dad."

'So much for damsels in distress,' Sir Tralahad thought as he rode away. 'No way am I writing about *her* for *Quest-O!*'

Just then an apple core clonked him on the back of the head.

Sir Tralahad was so upset, he had to stop and have a sandwich.

Chapter 4

The Dragon

Sir Prancelot went straight for the dragon, of course. No messing. It had been his idea to make the dragon the star of the whole quest and there was no way he was going home without the maximum 10 points, especially after those sharp words between him and Sir Gary.

Sir Prancelot liked to think he was a keen, happy sort of person who always looked on the bright side. Sir Gary was such a wet blanket. Sometimes, he really got on Sir Prancelot's nerves.

Sir Prancelot was sure that all the other knights would want to kill the dragon as well. He had to get there first.

He was headed for the mountain, which was a hard ride away, on the other side of the forest, and so he was very cross that he was stuck with Stop-A-Lot. He was on a proper forest path, with no speed limit and room for two-way traffic – but Stop-A-Lot was in no hurry at all. It was so very vexing!

Stop-A-Lot didn't care about speed. He ambled along, often stopping for a nibble, a scratch or to sniff a flower or admire a mushroom. If Stop-A-Lot had been human, he would have called everyone "man" and spent all his time in a hammock playing a mouth organ.

During one such stop something happened to change all this.

Stop-A-Lot had stopped to rub an itch he had on a tree. He leaned on the trunk and crushed Sir Prancelot's leg at the same time.

Sir Prancelot yanked at the reins and yelled a lot, and so he didn't hear the sound of hooves.

Sir Percy, on Gnasher, came thundering up the path.

Gnasher was mean and no one liked him. He had an evil temper and nipped anything that moved. Human, horse, dog, cat, anything that got near his nasty yellow teeth.

So it was that Gnasher gave Stop-A-Lot a nasty little bite – not bad enough to draw blood, but enough to hurt.

Sir Percy was green in the face from hanging on to Gnasher for grim death. There wasn't much you could do when riding Gnasher – he had to have his own way. Both horse and rider whooshed by and vanished into the forest. Sir Prancelot was left shocked and Stop-A-Lot was very fed up.

It took a lot to upset Stop-A-Lot. He was so chilled out that he put up with most things. But to get bitten for no reason at all was so not on, *man*.

He gave a little snort, showed the whites of his eyes and, to Sir Prancelot's surprise, set off after Gnasher. At top speed.

*

Everyone knew there was a dragon cave up the mountain. It was well known in the local village, which was called *Ye Dragon's Cave Village*. The cave was a major tourist attraction, along with a guided tour of the May Pole (in May only) and a visit to the village tea shop, which had a special medieval bun-and-boar meal deal on Saturdays.

The inn was called *Ye Dragon's Cave Inn* and the tea shop was *Ye Dragon's Cave Tea Shoppe*. A souvenir stall (*Ye Dragon's Cave Souvenirs*) sold soap dragons, blobby clay dragons and dragons carved very badly from wood.

A sign on the gate at the foot of the mountain read –

Danger! Ye Dragon's Cave.

The village made visitors sign a form to say it was all their own fault if they got burned by the dragon's flames, or eaten. They made them pay to go past the gate as well. A silver shilling, no less. That's why nobody ever went up to see the cave. It was a rip-off. Oh, there was a *cave* up there. But who knew if there was an actual *dragon* in it?

It was up to you – get ripped off, eaten or burned to a crisp. Better to stay at home.

Very few villagers were around that afternoon – just three old men on a bench in front of the inn. They were the only ones who saw Gnasher thunder up the village street with Sir Percy on his back.

Gnasher gave not a jot for danger signs, forms, silver shillings or gates. He didn't even

slow down. He just crashed past the gate and charged on up the mountain, kicking up dust.

The three old men watched the broken gate smash and fall into a heap.

Seconds later, Stop-A-Lot turned up with Sir Prancelot on his back, his long hair blowing in the wind. Stop-A-Lot didn't stop either. He just crashed past the broken gate and vanished in another cloud of dust.

The three old men stared in silence. After a bit, one of them said,

"Us'll need a new gate."

*

Like these things often are, the dragon's cave was a let-down. It was just a hole in the side of a cliff. You would have ridden past if it wasn't for the rock fall that blocked your way and forced you to stop.

That, and the big red arrow painted on the rock above the cave that said –

DRAGON'S CAVE.

Gnasher thundered round the bend, saw the rock fall and came to a sudden stop. Sir Percy flew over his head with a little scream and a big metal CRUNCH.

"Arrrhhh ..." Sir Percy gasped, flat on his back and out of breath. "Ow. That *hurt*." He would have laid there longer but Gnasher's terrible yellow teeth loomed over him.

"Oh no you don't, you monster," Sir Percy said, and he rolled over to one side. He staggered to his feet, put his helmet straight and wagged his finger at Gnasher.

"You are a *very* naughty horse!" he said. "Do that again and it will be old bread for you, for *one whole week*. I mean it, mind!"

Gnasher swished his tail, turned his back, lowered his head and started ripping into some grass.

Sir Percy stood for a moment, calmed himself down and took a deep breath. It didn't look good to lose control of your horse and fall off. At least there was no one around to see. That was something.

Except that there was. Wisps of green smoke were coming from the cave. Something was moving in there. In the smoke.

Sir Percy drew his sword.

At that very moment, Sir Prancelot cantered up on Stop-A-Lot.

Stop-A-Lot saw Gnasher, stopped and gave him a You Went Too Far Man look.

Gnasher stopped eating grass and gave him a Couldn't Care Less Pal stare.

Sir Prancelot jumped down, took out his sword and dashed over to Sir Percy, who didn't exactly look pleased to see him.

"What ho?" Sir Prancelot said, all excited. "Is there one in there? Is there? Is there? Did you see it?"

"I don't know," Sir Percy said. "Perhaps I saw something. Nothing to do with you. Run along, I'll sort it out."

"What d'you mean?" Sir Prancelot asked. "Why should *I* run along? I said I was jolly well doing the dragon. It was my idea!"

"No it wasn't," Sir Percy said. "You just said it first. Anyway, I'm here before you."

"I protest, sir!" Sir Prancelot cried. "No way will I back down on this."

"You have to," said Sir Percy. "This is a solo quest. *No questing in pairs* and all that. Every man for himself. I got here first and I will slay the mighty beast!"

"Is that so?" Sir Prancelot snapped. "Well, so will I. So we'll jolly well have to fight for – oh."

He broke off. The beast itself was now sitting in the cave entrance.

It was a dragon all right. But a tiny one. A sweet little dragon, about the size of a small stool. It was a bit like a lizard, with green scales, neatly folded wings and big golden-brown eyes. Puffs of green smoke rose from its nostrils. It had a cute gap in its teeth. Its stubby tail wagged in a friendly but shy way.

Sir Percy and Sir Prancelot both put their swords away.

"Ahhh," Sir Percy said. With a clank, he bent down and spoke softly, so as not to scare the little dragon. "Who is *dis*, den?"

"Can't say I was expecting this." Sir Prancelot had a soppy grin on his face. "Jolly cute little thing, isn't it?"

The dragon waggled its tiny tail then ran forward and jumped on Sir Percy's metal foot as if it wanted to play.

"Awwww," Sir Percy and Sir Prancelot said together.

The baby dragon made little growling noises. Then it rolled over and paddled its sweet little feet in the air.

"Just a baby," Sir Percy said.

"Coochy coo," Sir Prancelot said as he tickled its scaly green tummy.

Even the horses were charmed. Their eyes followed the little dragon as it toddled about. It gave happy little jumps, flapped its dinky little wings and almost, but not quite, flew up in the air.

"I wonder if it likes peacock and pickle sandwiches?" Sir Prancelot said. "I've still got half the last pack left."

"Try it," Sir Percy said. "If it doesn't like them, I've got boar and mustard."

Sir Prancelot ran to get the sandwiches from the saddlebags. The two horses ignored him. They were too much in love with the baby dragon.

The baby dragon liked the peacock and pickle sandwich, which it ate from Sir Prancelot's hand. It liked the boar and mustard too, which it ate from Sir Percy's hand. When it had finished, it climbed into Sir Percy's lap and started to purr. Sir Percy patted its trusting head.

"Do you think it's got a stack of treasure in there?" Sir Prancelot said as he stared into the dark cave.

"I don't think so. It's too little to look after treasure, isn't it?"

"It is. Too little to be here all on its own," said Sir Prancelot. Little green smoke rings rose from the dragon as it gently snored. "Anything could happen."

"Right," Sir Percy agreed. "Too little to be away from its mother."

There was a long silence as they both thought about this.

That was when a sound came from inside the cave. A low rumbling, growling sound along with a mass of thick green smoke. The ground shook and pebbles rose from the front of the cave.

Sir Percy and Sir Prancelot looked at each other.

The two horses looked at each other.

Sir Percy jumped up, spilling the baby dragon from his lap, and ran for Gnasher. He crashed into Sir Prancelot, who was making a dash for Stop-A-Lot.

"RUN!" they both screeched as they scrambled into their saddles.

Neither horse needed telling.

Behind them, two huge, angry red eyes looked out from a thick swirl of green smoke.

Chapter 5

Swords

Sir Bore de Gannet's first choice of good deed was the damsel in distress. It would win him a lot of points, *and* it was his sort of thing. Ladies, towers, romantic speeches in a French accent – he could see it all. But that was before he got Loud Winnie.

Loud Winnie was a bag of nerves. Anything and everything gave her the jitters – a dropped sandwich, a funny-shaped tree, a cloud, a sudden bird call.

Every two seconds, she jumped in the air,
all four hooves off the ground, to let out a shrill
screech that bore into the head like a drill. The
only way to calm Loud Winnie down was to
take her somewhere safe and give her a quiet
drink of warm milk.

Loud Winnie was a very, very tiring horse
to ride, cotton wool ear plugs or no.

Sir Bore de Gannet had only ridden for five
minutes or so when he knew that he couldn't
go on. In those five minutes, Loud Winnie
had freaked out at a squirrel, a puddle, a bee,
a twig, a banana skin, a butterfly, a falling
leaf and her own shadow (two times). It was
impossible. Just not worth the aggro.

So – a change of plan.

Sir Bore de Gannet decided to stay local
rather than riding miles looking for a damsel.
He would try his luck with a sword. A sword
stuck in a stone would earn the most points,
but he couldn't think of any big stones close by.

But there was a pond not that far away. A nice little pond, with frogs and lily pads. The knights sometimes went fishing there on hot days. It wasn't exactly a lake, but it was –

1. **Wet**
and
2. **Close by**.

It was somewhere to park Loud Winnie, sit on the handy log at the pond's edge and watch for any hands with swords to rise from the water. Unlikely, but not impossible.

And it would be a nice place for lunch. Sir Bore de Gannet was looking forward to lunch. Croissants would have been good, but Mrs Spunge's Olde English doorstopper sandwiches would do instead.

Only problem was that Sir Gary had had the same idea about the pond and was already there.

The whole quest thing was not Sir Gary's idea of fun. He thought quests were stupid. Too much effort. He would prefer to stay at home in the castle, sit around the drop-leaf table and moan his head off.

Lightning was the horse equivalent of Sir Gary. Lightning just couldn't be bothered. He'd prefer to be back in the stable moaning to the other horses. He was a born sulker. Nothing was good. Nothing was right. Carrots too soft or too crunchy. Hay too soggy or too dry. Stable too hot or too cold. No, Lightning didn't want to trek for miles on a warm day with some metal twit on his back. Why would he?

The minute they reached the forest, Sir Gary and Lightning made for the pond. It was easy. No effort. Find a shady spot and hang about until it was time to go home. Eat the sandwiches – or grass – both of which would be rubbish. Spend a surly hour chucking stones in the pond or kicking a tree. Maybe a hand would show up out of the water with a sword. Or maybe not. Who cared?

So it was that Sir Bore de Gannet and Loud Winnie came across Sir Gary and Lightning already in the best spot.

Sir Gary was on the fallen log and Lightning under a nice shady tree. Both of them looked very fed up when they saw Sir Bore de Gannet and Loud Winnie.

"So, Sir Gary!" Sir Bore de Gannet called out over the screeches of Loud Winnie, who was in a big tizz at the unexpected meeting. "What are you doing 'ere? Could it be – Sword Watching?"

Sir Gary gave a shrug and bit into his first sandwich. He shuffled along into the middle of the log and spread out his metal knees to show that he wasn't prepared to share the only seat.

"I just want you to know, sir," Sir Bore de Gannet went on as he got down from Loud

Winnie, "zat if a sword appears from out of ze water, it 'as my name on it. You may as well give up now."

Sir Gary finished chewing, gulped and said, "No way. I asked for royal swan. This is griffin salad."

"Did you 'ear me? Ze sword is mine, I say!"

"Why don't you put a sock in it?" Sir Gary said, and he squashed the sandwich in its wrapper and threw it in the pond.

"I saw zat!" Sir Bore de Gannet jumped into fighting mode, hand on his sword. "Zat goes against ze Code! You are – 'ow you say – Engleesh litter lout!"

"Yeah, yeah," Sir Gary said. "I thought you were doing the distressed damsel? Changed your mind, have you?"

"As a matter of fact, I 'ave. Now, I go for ze sword."

"You know what?" Sir Gary put his hand into the saddlebag, took out all the sandwiches and chucked them in the pond, where they sank like stones. "Have it. It's all yours, mate. I'm off 'ome. Bloomin' griffin salad, my foot. Get myself some proper hot food. Don't envy you later, when it's dark."

Sir Gary took Lightning by the reins and together, without looking back, they walked away towards the castle.

Sir Bore de Gannet was shocked. It was so un-knightly to give up and sneak off back home. The Best Quest was supposed to last three days, not an afternoon.

But it didn't have to, of course. Nobody had said it couldn't end sooner.

And Sir Gary had done it now. So he, Sir Bore de Gannet, wouldn't be the first.

Of course, there was his pride as a knight. He should make the effort to win lots of points and beat the others. There was a proper prize too. A fine old silver goblet, from Her Majesty, no less.

But to sword watch all afternoon. Could he stand it? And Sir Gary was right. He wouldn't be able to see a thing in the dark.

Sir Bore de Gannet wasn't sure, but – wasn't that a drop of rain?

That was it. He was decided. It wouldn't do to let his armour rust.

*

"Hear that? What did I say?" Old Toby said to Shawn.

They were in the stable yard, just about to have a cuppa, a slice of cake and a game of cards. Bob the dog was sitting in a pile of straw. Ethel the cat was on the wall washing her whiskers.

They could hear the sound of hooves in the lane.

"What – is that someone back already?" said Shawn. "They've only been gone an hour or two."

"Yep. Mark my words, he's eaten all the sandwiches."

Bob the dog wagged his tail. Ethel the cat flicked her ears, stood up, stretched, and rubbed up against a drain pipe in a pleased way. It was what they always did when they saw Sir Angela.

"It's Angela," said Shawn. "I mean, Sir AnGela."

"You're right," Old Toby said. "Here she comes. I mean he."

It was indeed Sir Angela, a very quiet Sir Angela. She muttered about feeling a spot of rain and not wanting her armour to go rusty.

She handed over Elton (after a pat on the nose) and clanked away. Bob wagged along at her heels and Ethel strolled behind.

"Seems a bit down in the dumps," said Old Toby.

Sir Angela was indeed down in the dumps. She was the first back, which was a bad show. She was starving, because she'd only had one sandwich all day. The wise woman had stolen the rest from her saddlebag. In return, all Sir Angela had was a few dry stalks and a pocket full of dust. Perhaps a long time ago it was a bunch of lucky white heather. Whatever. Angela didn't think it would count as proof.

Sad to say, she had won no points.

Should she go straight to her room and sulk? Or go to the kitchen for a snack? A bit of Mrs Spunge's cake would be nice.

*

Shortly after, Sir Tralahad arrived in the stable yard, tired and not singing, for once.

He too muttered something about rain and his armour. He handed over Breakwind and clunked off to the castle without a word. He had no note from a damsel in distress. Nothing from the damsel at all, apart from a dent in his helmet. And it had been an embarrassing mistake about the hair. He really would have to visit Knight Vision and get an eye test. And he hadn't got any further with his *Quest-O!* song.

No points for Sir Tralahad.

*

Sir Percy and Sir Prancelot showed up next.

For some reason, they smelled a bit burned, as if they'd been near a camp fire. But they didn't say anything about it. They just murmured about damp in the air that might turn to rain – the armour, you know – handed over Gnasher and Stop-A-Lot, and walked off stiffly. The entire dragon thing had been very embarrassing for them both. They didn't want to talk about it.

Anyway. No points for them.

*

Sir Gary showed up next, with a face like a kite.

He didn't say anything about rain or armour. He and Lightning parted at the gate and went their separate ways, glad to see the back of each other. To Sir Gary's mind, the quest thing had been a total waste of time.

No points for him, then.

As if he cared.

*

Last of all – because Loud Winnie had played up – came Sir Bore de Gannet.

Loud Winnie only stopped screeching when she entered the yard. Sir Bore de Gannet got down, muttered in French about *la pluie* and *l'armure* and scuttled out of the yard. No magic sword to show for his efforts. Not that he had made any effort.

Nul points.

*

That left Old Toby and Shawn to take off all the saddles, bridles, stirrups, feathers, tassels, bells, whistles and other finery from six sweaty, grubby horses. Then they had to rub them down and feed them hay and water. Instead of having their own tea and a game of cards, that is.

Medieval life just wasn't fair.

Epilogue

It was three nights later and the King and Queen were having a bedtime mug of hot chocolate in the throne room.

"So, Gwinny," the King said. "How did the award ceremony go this evening? That Best Quest thing the knights dreamed up. It was tonight, wasn't it?"

"Yes," said the Queen. "It was. I went down with the silver goblet, as promised. They were all expecting me. Had a welcome banner and extra candles. It's the first time I've been to the new room. They've got it looking nice, but that table's not great. It slopes on the drop-leaf side."

"Yes, dear," the King said. "But who won the goblet?"

"Well – nobody."

"What d'you mean, nobody? It was a quest to see who was best, wasn't it?"

"Well, yes. But it was all so complicated, Artie. All this business of points for this and points for that. They tried to explain it, but I just couldn't take it in. And there had to be proof that they'd done what they said they had, and there wasn't any proof except for a handful of dust from Sir AnGela. She – he – he said it was lucky heather in return for a kind deed, but everyone said it was just dirt and it wasn't proper proof. And they wouldn't let her – I mean him – have points for returning lost pets to their owners either."

"What lost pets?" the King asked.

"Bob and Ethel. Sir AnGela brought them back to the kitchen and gave them to Mrs Spunge."

"But they weren't lost. They live here."

"That's what the others said. So Sir AnGela didn't win the points."

"So," King Artie said with a sigh, "what were they doing on the quest for three days?"

"It wasn't three days, it was just Monday afternoon. And I don't know. Nobody would talk about it. Anyway, the result was that nobody won and they told me to hang on to the silver goblet until the next time."

"Oh dear. Rather an anti-climax."

"You're right, Artie, it was." Queen Gwinny took a big sip of her rather cold hot chocolate. "After they'd stopped shouting about points and who'd got the worst horse, it all went a bit flat. They seemed – a bit low. So I asked Mrs Spunge to take them that leftover trifle from tea. And I sent Aggie along with that box of chocolates that the King of Italy sent us. It's too big for just the two of us. I hope it cheers them up."

"Darling," the King said. "It's sure to. You are such a treasure. Cheers!"

And they clinked together their mugs and drank.

The Ballad of the Girl with Attitude
A Song of Freedom by Sir Tralahad

The damsel I tried to set free, hey ho,
Was not in distress all along,
She was ever so nasty to me, hey ho,
And she doesn't belong in my song.

Her attitude's wrong,
She doesn't belong,
She doesn't belong in my song, oh no.

I sing about bunnies and flowers, hey ho,
And rainbows and sunshine and showers,
And butterfly wings and beautiful things,
Not potty-mouthed maidens in towers.

With a hey nonny no,
The girl's got to go,
I'm kicking her out of my song!

Our books are tested
for children and young people by
children and young people.

Thanks to everyone who consulted on
a manuscript for their time and effort in
helping us to make our books better
for our readers.